The Three Little Pigs
and other bedtime stories

Contents

ARCTURUS

The Three Little Pigs

Once upon a time,
there were three little pigs
who lived with their mother.

The day came when they
decided to set out to find homes
of their own.

"Remember to look out for the
Big Bad Wolf," said their mother.

It wasn't long before they met
a man with a load of straw.

"I could build a very good house with that straw," said the first little pig and he bought the lot. He worked hard and by dinnertime, he had built himself a very snug little house.

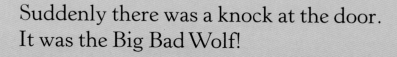

Suddenly there was a knock at the door. It was the Big Bad Wolf!

"Little pig, little pig, let me come in!" called the wolf.

"No, no, by the hair on my chinny chin chin, I will not let you in!" said the first little pig.

"Then I'll huff and I'll puff and
I'll blow your house down!"
growled the wolf.

 The Big, Bad Wolf took a deep breath.
He huffed and he puffed and he blew the house
down! The first little pig ran off as fast
as his trotters could carry him.

Meanwhile, the second and third
little pigs had walked on down the
winding road. Soon they met
a man with a load of sticks.

"I could make myself a very
good house with those sticks,"
said the second little pig.

He waved goodbye to his sister and before long, he had built a snug little house.

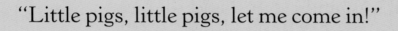

Suddenly there came a knock at the door. It was the first little pig!

"Let me in!" he cried. "The Big, Bad Wolf is close behind me!"

"Little pigs, little pigs, let me come in!"

"No, no, by the hair on our chinny chin chins," replied the two little pigs, "we will not let you in!"

"Then I'll huff and I'll puff and I'll blow your house down!" The Big, Bad Wolf took a deep breath and he huffed, and he puffed and he blew the house down!

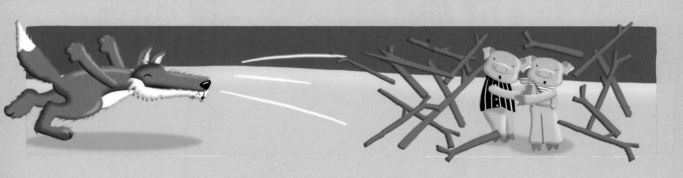

Meanwhile, the third little pig had met a man
with a cart full of bricks and she had quickly
built a lovely house.

Suddenly, there came a hammering at the door.
"Let us in, let us in!" cried her brothers.
"The Big, Bad Wolf is on his way!"

It wasn't long before they heard the wolf outside.
"Little pigs, little pigs, let me come in!"

"No, no, by the hair on our chinny chin chins,"
chorused the three little pigs, "we will not
let you in!"

"Then I'll huff and I'll puff and I'll blow
your house down!" fumed the wolf.

He huffed and he puffed. The brick house stood strong and true. Now the wolf was really angry.

"He's trying to climb down the chimney!" whispered the girl pig. "Help me with this pot!"

The pigs dragged a huge pot on to the fire and filled it with water. By the time the wolf had squeezed himself down the chimney, the pot was boiling and he dipped his tail in the hot water.

"Yeeeeeoowwww!" he yelled. That Big, Bad Wolf shot straight up the chimney and off down the road. He was never seen again, and the three little pigs lived happily ever after.

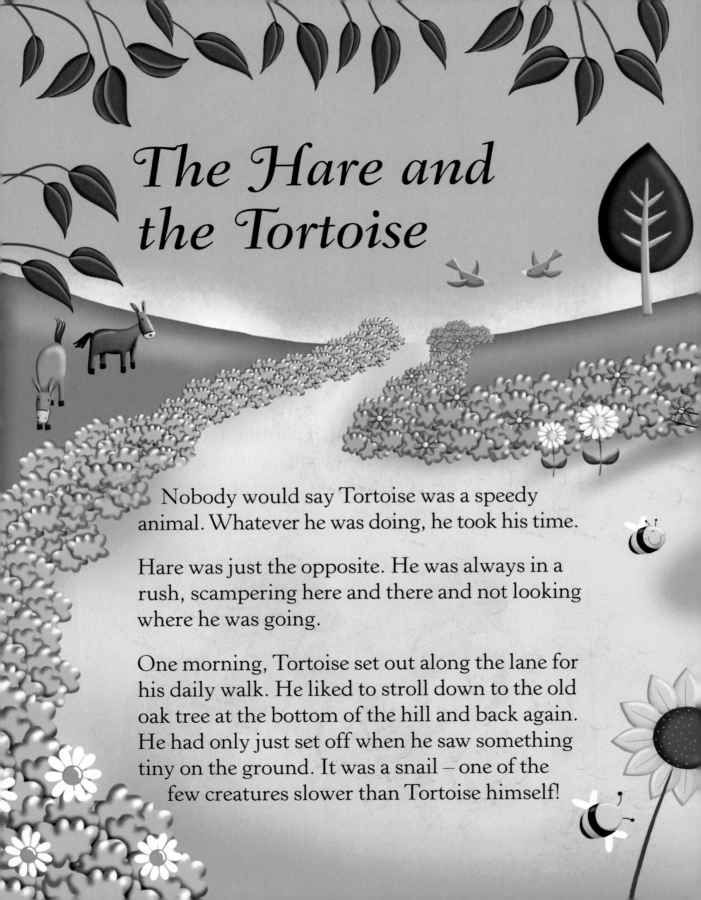

The Hare and the Tortoise

Nobody would say Tortoise was a speedy animal. Whatever he was doing, he took his time.

Hare was just the opposite. He was always in a rush, scampering here and there and not looking where he was going.

One morning, Tortoise set out along the lane for his daily walk. He liked to stroll down to the old oak tree at the bottom of the hill and back again. He had only just set off when he saw something tiny on the ground. It was a snail – one of the few creatures slower than Tortoise himself!

At that moment, Hare came hurtling up the hill. BUMP! Poor Tortoise spun right round in the road.

The surprise left Hare speechless for a moment, which gave Tortoise a chance to speak up.

"You really must be more careful, Hare," he said in his usual slow way. "You'll never get anywhere rushing around like you do."

Hare laughed, "I'll get farther than you, old slowpoke," he chortled. "Are you going to the oak tree? I could go there and be back at your house before you got started."

"I don't think you could, you know," said Tortoise.

"That sounds like a challenge!" yelled Hare,
bouncing about in the road now.
"Let's have a race!"

"Fair enough," said Tortoise, slowly.

Off zoomed Hare. He was out of sight in
seconds. Tortoise plodded on, just as he
always did.

Meanwhile, Hare was dashing down the lane,
so full of himself that he jumped and skipped
as he went. By the time he reached the oak tree,
he was out of breath.

"I'll just sit down here for a minute," said Hare to
himself. "It will take all morning for Tortoise to
get here. I've got plenty of time."

The sun was warm. Before long, Hare began to feel drowsy and soon he began to snore.

When Tortoise came slowly into view half an hour later, Hare was still asleep. Tortoise didn't say a word. He just kept walking.

It was lunchtime when Hare woke up and remembered the race. He jumped to his feet and shot off down the lane. There was no sign of Tortoise.

Hare ran faster than he had ever run before – that's pretty fast! He skidded to a stop outside Tortoise's house. To his horror, the door opened and the slow old creature appeared.

"Wah? Hah? How?" panted Hare.

"Slow and steady wins the race," said Tortoise, slowly and steadily. "Come on in."

The Little Red Hen

There was once a little red hen who lived with her friends on a farm. One day, she found some ears of wheat that had fallen from the farmer's truck. She didn't eat them right away, for as soon as she saw them, she had an idea.

"Who will help me plant this wheat?" she asked her friends.

"Well, I won't," said the cat.

"Nor will I," said the rat.

"I simply can't," said the pig.

"Then I'll do it myself,"
said the little red hen.
And she did.

The tiny grains of wheat
grew and grew into tall
stems with ripe ears of
wheat at the top.
The little red hen saw
that the wheat was
ready to be cut.

"Who will help me harvest
the wheat?" she asked.

"Well, I won't," said the cat.

"Nor will I," said the rat.

"I simply can't," said the pig.

"Then I'll do it myself," said the little red hen.
And she did.

"Who will help me take the
wheat to the mill to be ground into flour?"
asked the little red hen.

"Well, I won't," said the cat.

"Nor will I," said the rat.

"I simply can't," said the pig.

"Then I'll do it myself," said the little red hen.
And she did.

"Who will help me make some bread with this
flour?" she asked her friends.

"Well, I won't," said the cat.

"Nor will I," said the rat.

"I simply can't," said the pig.

"Then I'll do it myself," said the little red hen.
And she did.

Soon a wonderful smell came from the
farmhouse kitchen. The bread was ready!

"Who will help me to eat my delicious bread?"
called the little red hen.

"Well, I will!" said the cat.

"So will I!" said the rat.

"I simply can't wait!"
said the pig.

The little red hen
saw that the cat and
the rat and the pig were
not really friends at all.

"No," she said, "I think
I'll eat it myself."
And she did.

The Other Frog Prince

One evening, as the stars began to shine, Mother Frog read her froglets the story of the Frog Prince. "The Princess kissed the frog," she told her three children, "and at once he turned into a handsome Prince.

The Prince and the Princess were married
and lived happily ever after." Young Fiona Frog
and Little Freddie Frog giggled and settled
down on their lily pads. But Felix Frog was too
excited to sleep. There and then, he decided
he would find a beautiful Princess, turn into a
handsome Prince, and marry her.

As soon as he was old enough, Felix set out
to make his dream come true. He hopped to a
beautiful pink castle and there in the grounds
was a real Princess. She was certainly beautiful,
but she looked bored and unhappy.

"She looks sad because she hasn't met me yet,"
said Felix to himself. He knew that it might
be difficult to persuade the Princess that he
was really a Prince in disguise, so he hopped
into a flowerbed and made himself a little crown
from a golden flower.

Felix approached the Princess. He saw that
she was holding a small picture of a young
man. From time to time, she leaned down
and kissed it with tears in her eyes.

Now Felix knew what to do.

Instead of persuading the Princess to kiss him,
he simply hopped on to the picture and waited.
Sure enough, the Princess sighed, puckered up
her lips and leaned down.

"Eeeeeuuuurgh!" She flung the picture from her.
"Help! Eeeeeeuuuurgh! A dirty frog is on my
picture of Prince Goodheart!" she shrieked.

Just then, the young man in the picture hurtled through a nearby hedge and swept the Princess up into his arms.

"I will save you, beloved!" he cried. "Forgive me for taking so long to return. I had trouble with my carriage."

While the Princess kissed her Prince, Felix hopped hurriedly away. His dreams were shattered. When he saw a pool of cool, shimmering water before him, he dived in with relief. He began to feel more like himself again.

A silvery voice interrupted him. "You've lost your crown, your Highness," said a charming young girl-frog, who was sitting on a lily leaf. She was holding his flower crown and wearing something similar herself. "I'm … I'm not a Prince," stammered Felix, "not really."

"I'm not a Princess," smiled the new frog kindly, "but it's nice to pretend, isn't it?"

Felix blurted out, "You're certainly pretty enough to be a Princess!"

The end of this story is easy to tell.
The Frog Princess kissed Felix and at once he became the handsome frog of her dreams.
The Frog Princess and her Frog Prince were married and lived happily ever after.

Moon Magic

Over the hills and far away, in the middle
of a forest, there lived an owl family.
They were Father Owl, Mother Owl, and Little
Egg. A hole in a mighty oak tree was their home.

One day, Little Egg gently cracked open and someone very fluffy came out.

"Whooo is this?" asked Father Owl, looking down at the bundle of fluff.

"It is Little Owl," said Mother Owl. "He is here at last."

Each night, Father Owl flew off to find food for them all. When Little Owl grew bigger, he needed even more food! Mother Owl flew off as well to find enough for the family.

When he was all alone,
Little Owl got scared.
Something big and round
was shining down at him.

"Ooooo!" said Little Owl.

When he told Mother Owl, she hooted
with laughter. "It's the mooooon," she said.
"It is magic. Each night, it shines down and
keeps owls safe. When Father Owl and I are not
here, the magic moon will look after you."

That made Little Owl feel better. That night,
he shuffled to the edge of the hole and looked
up at the moon. It was looking down,
making sure he was safe.

Little Owl was getting older now. He did a lot of thinking about things. After a few days, he found something new to worry about. He noticed that the moon was beginning to disappear. At first, he wasn't sure, but after a while he saw that each night there was a little bit less of the moon.

He wasn't sure if there was enough moon left to keep him safe each night.

Night by night,
the moon got smaller
and smaller,
until it was just
a silver sliver
in the sky.

That night, Little Owl begged his
mother not to go out.

"I have to go, Little Owl," she said, "or you
will be hungry. You know that the magic moon
will look after you."

"It isn't magic," said Little Owl sadly.
"Something has been nibbling away at it.
Last night there was hardly any
moon. Tonight it won't be
there at all."

"Nooooooo, Little Owl," smiled his mother. "That's why the moon is magic. Each month, it gets smaller and smaller night after night, until it is a tiny sliver. Then it begins to grow again, until one night it is big and round once more."

Little Owl wasn't sure, but he knew that his mother was very wise. Sure enough, over the next few nights the moon began to grow.

By the time the magic moon was big again, Little Owl was quite big, too. He understood lots of things now. Safe in the forest up in the oak tree, on a branch near the hole, he smiled at the moon. And the moon smiled back.

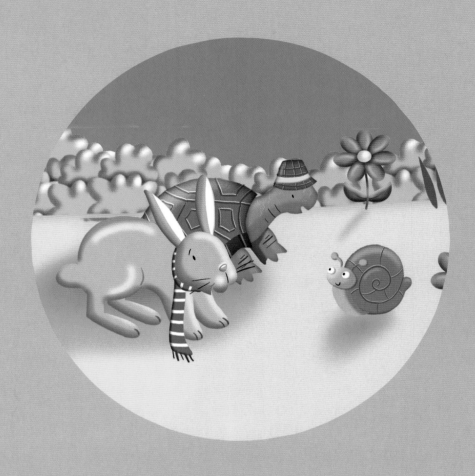

This edition published in 2014 by Arcturus Publishing Limited
26/27 Bickels Yard, 151–153 Bermondsey Street,
London SE1 3HA

ISBN: 978-1-84858-866-0
CH002600NT
Supplier 15, Date 0114, Print run 2979

Printed in China